Beast Quest ®

Fluger
The Sightless
Slitherer

BY ADAM BLADE

ORCHARD

With special thanks to Allan Frewin Jones

For Zachary Nasralla.
Never forget you are the hero of your own story.
Enjoy all the adventures ahead.

www.beastquest.co.uk

ORCHARD BOOKS

First published in Great Britain in 2019 by The Watts Publishing Group

1 3 5 7 9 10 8 6 4 2

Text © 2019 Beast Quest Limited.
Cover and inside illustrations by Steve Sims
© Beast Quest Limited 2019

Beast Quest is a registered trademark of Beast Quest Limited
Series created by Beast Quest Limited, London

A CIP catalogue record for this book is available from the British Library.

ISBN 978 1 40835 777 4

Printed in Great Britain

The paper and board used in this book are made from wood from responsible sources

Orchard Books
An imprint of Hachette Children's Group
Part of The Watts Publishing Group Limited
Carmelite House, 50 Victoria Embankment, London EC4Y 0DZ

An Hachette UK Company
www.hachette.co.uk
www.hachettechildrens.co.uk

Welcome to the world of Beast Quest!

Tom was once an ordinary village boy, until he travelled to the City, met King Hugo and discovered his destiny. Now he is the Master of the Beasts, sworn to defend Avantia and its people against Evil. Tom draws on the might of the magical Golden Armour, and is protected by powerful tokens granted to him by the Good Beasts of Avantia. Together with his loyal companion Elenna, Tom is always ready to visit new lands and tackle the enemies of the realm.

While there's blood in his veins, Tom will never give up the Quest…

There are special gold coins to collect in this book. You will earn one coin for every chapter you read.

Find out what to do with your coins at the end of the book.

CONTENTS

Banners fly from the walls of King Hugo's Palace and all Avantia rejoices at Tom's latest victory. The people worship the snivelling wretch as if he's their saviour.

Well, forgive me if I'm not bowing down. He killed my father Sanpao and drove my mother Kensa from the kingdom.

So, in revenge, I'm going to spoil their little party.

Soon Avantia will face a Beast like no other.

And when they look for their little hero to save their skins, he will be nowhere to be found.

Ria

A FRIEND IN NEED

"Daltec!"

Elenna crouched beside the wizard. His eyes were closed, but he was breathing. After the battle with Electro the Storm Bird, the young witch Ria had fired a magical ball of energy at Daltec from her winged horse. Moments later, Tom had climbed up behind Ria and they had

flown off into the empty desert skies
of Pyloris.

"Wake up!" Elenna urged.

One of the desert people came
close, kneeling and holding a spiky
flower under Daltec's nose. "It will

revive him," he explained.

The wizard spluttered and coughed. His eyes opened wide and he sat up.

"The token?" he said weakly. "Where is Electro's feather?"

"It's too late," Elenna told him,

pointing into the endless desert. "Tom gave it to Ria! They've already gone."

Daltec's shoulders slumped. Elenna felt exactly the same way. This was a Quest like no other, for it was the first time she didn't have Tom at her side. Since donning his enchanted armour, he'd been infected with the blood of Krokol, an ancient Beast. It had turned his soul to Evil and he'd teamed up with their enemy Ria.

Daltec stood up. He seemed to sense Elenna's misery, and rested his hand on her arm. "There is still Good in him," he said. "Once we give him Aduro's antidote, he will be the old Tom again."

Elenna nodded, trying to heed Daltec's words. One of the elders of the desert tribe approached them, dressed in ceremonial robes and with a wreath of bones around his forehead.

"You have proved yourselves worthy," he said, his voice as dry and cracked as the desert wind. "We are free now from the curse of Electro. But there are two more of Krokol's spawn out there."

Elenna nodded. When Tanner, Tom's ancestor, defeated Krokol, the deadly giant was separated into three Beasts. Elenna wasn't sure why Ria was intent on killing the Beasts, but the fact that she was using Tom to do so made Elenna's skin crawl. Ria didn't care about Tom's life at all, and there was every chance he would be killed doing Ria's bidding.

Elenna took out a compass and held it on her palm. It belonged to Tom and had helped him on many quests, but Daltec had replaced the needle with a splinter from the helmet of Tom's enchanted armour. It was tainted by the blood of Krokol too, and would always point to Tom's location.

The needle spun then came to rest, pointing out across the barren desert. The elder shook his head. "That way leads only to the Bone

Sands," he told them. "None who go that way survive."

"All the same, we must follow the compass," Elenna replied. "I've got to

find my friend."

The elder nodded wisely, as though he could sense the determination in Elenna's heart. They mounted Storm, Elenna taking the reins while Daltec clung on behind. Having said goodbye, she nudged the stallion's flanks and he broke into a trot.

As they left the shelter of the pyramid of Electro behind, a hot gusting breeze kicked up the sand around them, and Elenna had to tie a cloth over her mouth and nose, squinting her eyes. All she could see was sand, blurring in a heat haze to the horizon.

We've got to trust the compass,

she told herself. *Tom needs me more than he has ever done before. I won't let him down!*

THE BONE SANDS

The wind whipped through the red bristles of Ria's mohawk as Tom sat behind her, his eyes narrowed against the blazing sun. Sweat ran down his face and his ears were filled with the steady flapping of the flying horse's huge wings.

Below them, the ground sped away, empty of life and scarred by fissures and gaping chasms.

Tom guessed that his new mistress had used the Lightning Staff to travel to Henkrall – where all creatures and people had wings. He wondered if the stallion had been a wild animal, or if she'd stolen it from someone. Not that he really cared. His blood still burned from the battle with Electro. There was nothing like seeing a Beast vanquished!

"You know, Tom," shouted Ria above the wind, "I expected more of you. If it wasn't for Elenna's arrow, you might be dead now."

"A lucky shot," he grumbled.

But the mention of Elenna sent a

lance of pain through his heart. He found himself thinking of the girl, and her wizard friend. He wondered how they were faring, and why she had saved his life. Old memories drifted to his mind. It wasn't the first time she'd acted so selflessly. *That's right. She's my friend…it's Ria who's my enemy.*

Glancing down, his eyes fell on the green-hilted dagger in Ria's belt.

All he had to do was take it. Hold it to her throat and force her to land.

He reached out trembling fingers towards the dagger.

"Seriously, Tom?" Ria said in a mocking voice. "Go on – take the dagger, I won't stop you." She

laughed. "You can't harm me. You
would cut your own throat before
you were able to spill a single drop
of my blood."

Her words made his mind swirl with fog. Tom drew his hand back. The agony across his heart drained away, leaving only blackness.

What was I thinking?

"I'm sorry," he said.

"Are you loyal to me, Tom?" Ria asked, glancing at him over her shoulder. "Would you die for me?"

"Yes," Tom breathed. "Always!"

"That's a good boy."

Her laughter filled his ears, but he didn't mind – he deserved her mockery. He must do better – he must prove his loyalty.

And if Elenna or Daltec try and stop me, I'll cut them down without mercy.

Tom lost track of how long they had been in the air. The desolate landscape flowed away beneath them, nothing but rocks and sand and parched earth. The burning sun moved slowly across the sky and the wind scorched his face and tore at his hair.

"Aha!" Ria flicked the reins and the flying horse began to descend.

Tom looked over her shoulder. Ahead of them, he saw a small derelict village, huddled mournfully in a dry hollow.

Shortly, the horse came to a cantering landing. Ria tugged on the reins and the horse folded its wings and walked slowly in among the crumbling mud-brick huts.

What a miserable place! No wonder it's deserted!

They dismounted, and Ria patted the horse's neck. "Stay close," she whispered in its ear.

The horse huffed through its nose. Then it gave a great leap and soared into the air.

"Come on, Tom – we have work to do," said Ria, leading him towards one of the huts. It was half-buried in sand, its walls cracked and uneven.

"I don't see what business we could have in such a place," said Tom.

"Lucky I don't need you for your

opinions," muttered Ria.

She kicked at the rotten wooden door and it swung open to reveal a flight of dusty steps that plunged into the ground. Tom followed her

into the cold darkness. As the light
dwindled, Ria muttered a spell
and a greenish light grew at her
fingertips.

"There's a network of water
tunnels under the desert here," she
told him. "The locals dug them to
provide drinking water and for
shelter from the sandstorms. That
was before Fluger arrived."

"Fluger?" whispered Tom. "Is that
the next of Krokol's offspring?"

"So I've heard," said Ria. "They
call him the Sightless Slitherer."

They reached the foot of the stairs
and a tunnel. "It might be best for
you to walk in front of me," Ria said.
"You don't mind, do you?"

"Not at all." Tom passed her in the narrow passageway.

I am Ria's champion – of course I should face the Beast first!

"That's my noble hero," chuckled Ria.

They walked on, but Tom began to feel uneasy. The light from Ria's fingers threw his shadow along the tunnel, making it hard for him to see the way ahead. Brittle things cracked under his feet.

He looked down. The ground was scattered with bones. Some were only small, as though little creatures had scuttled in here for safety and had never found their way out again.

Then a more familiar shape grinned

up at Tom – a human skull!

People have died down here...

Cold air flowed up from hidden depths, like an icy breath.

Tom thought he heard something ahead. He stopped, listening intently.

"What is it?" Ria asked impatiently.

Skrrk. Skrrk. Skrrk.

It was the sound of something sharp scraping on stone.

"Stay back." Tom drew his sword. "There's something alive down here."

He peered into the gloom. The walls of the tunnel were scored with fissures, behind them and ahead.

Suddenly a dog-sized creature scuttled out from a crack.

Tom gasped and Ria let out a

squeal of fright.

It was a scorpion – a giant one!
Its armoured body was a greenish
yellow and its arched legs clicked on

the ground as it turned and moved towards Tom. Its pincers clacked as its curved tail rose above its back, the sting dripping yellow venom.

A second scorpion emerged from the wall, its pale eyes gleaming with hungry menace. Then there was a third.

Tom turned in alarm, hearing more scrabbling.

Three more scorpions were approaching them from behind.

We're trapped!

THE RAGING STORM

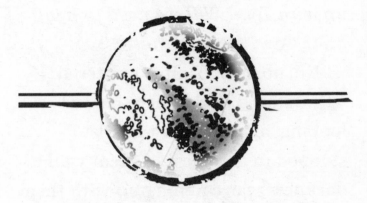

The desert seemed to stretch on for ever. Elenna leaned between Storm's ears, peering at the featureless horizon. The breath was hot in her lungs and the wind snatched and tore at her clothes.

She glanced down at the compass. The black needle pointed straight ahead – into the dead heart of the Bone Sands.

What will happen when we catch up with Tom? Will we need to fight him? Can I even do that?

"No, no, no…" Daltec muttered.

She stared back where he was looking, and her heart almost stopped in her chest. A great wall of darkness was catching up with them. Already it had eaten up a third of the sky, like an immense ocean wave.

"A sandstorm!" said Elenna.

"It's coming straight for us," said Daltec.

"We will outrun it!" Elenna declared, flicking the reins. "Come on, boy," she urged. "You can do it!"

"With a little help, maybe he can,"
said Daltec. He muttered a spell and
a glittering swirl of magical energy
coiled around Storm's legs.

Instantly, the stallion galloped

faster. Elenna was jerked back, then threw her body low over the horse. Storm's legs were a blur below. They covered the ground at an astonishing rate and for a moment they seemed to be pulling ahead of the sandstorm. But then the magic faded, and they slowed again.

"What happened?" Elenna asked.

"I…I don't know," Daltec replied.

The dark cloud of sand rushed upon them, just a few stinging grains at first, then a hail of choking particles. Daltec cried out as the sand wave came crashing down with a howling sound like a pack of monstrous wolves. Elenna felt herself torn from the saddle. She heard Storm whinny in fear, then tumbled head over heels, blinded and buffeted by the roaring storm. She crashed painfully to the ground, and a terrifying weight of sand hammered down on her back.

Coughing and choking, Elenna clawed her way up through the sand. She heaved herself out and lay gasping under the sweltering sun. She stared around in alarm. "Daltec!" she shouted. "Storm!"

Smooth sand dunes stretched away in every direction. There was no sign of her companions. She scrambled among the dunes, desperately calling their names. *No! They can't be dead!*

A whooshing sound startled her. A little way off, a sand-spout gushed

up from the side of a dune. With
a yell, Daltec shot into the air. He
somersaulted and crashed down on
his back.

Elenna scrambled over to where he was lying, his face red, his chest heaving. "Are you all right?" she gasped.

He blinked at her then smiled. "It took a powerful spell to get me out," he panted. "I think I overdid it slightly."

She helped him to his feet. "I can't find Storm," Elenna told him.

"Listen!" said Daltec. "What's that sound?"

Elenna heard a faint whinnying from beyond a hump-backed dune. They rushed over. Storm's head was visible in the sand, straining back as he fought to get free.

Daltec dug around the terrified

stallion while Elenna heaved on Storm's reins to help him clamber out of the sand. Storm whickered and shook his head, his ears flat and his eyes rolling.

Elenna led the horse to the top of the dune. Far away she could see something that looked like a rock formation. She studied the compass. "It's leading us towards those rocks," she told Daltec.

As they came closer, Elenna realised it was not a natural formation at all. It was an abandoned village of crumbling brick huts.

They dismounted and walked in among the broken buildings.

The needle of the compass began to sway back and forth.

"What does this mean?" Elenna asked, showing the spinning needle to Daltec, who frowned. "It's like the compass is confused."

"Or Tom is beneath us," Daltec said, pointing at the ground.

Elenna spotted what looked like an old well. "Could there be tunnels?"

"Maybe so," said Daltec. They hurried to the well and stared down its parched throat. Elenna picked up a stone and lobbed it in. Seconds passed before a hollow thud echoed up.

"It's deep," she said. "And empty." She gave Daltec a determined look.

"We have to go down there."

Daltec bit his lip. "If we must."

Elenna climbed over the rim of the
well. She cautiously lowered herself
in, bracing her back against the wall
and finding footholds opposite.

Slowly, she began to descend, using hands and feet and keeping her back tight to the brickwork. Daltec climbed in after her, blotting out a good deal of light.

A chunk of brick came loose under Elenna's foot and tumbled away, crashing against the walls until it thumped to the ground far, far below. Her heart pounded.

One wrong move and this Quest is over...

4

PERIL IN THE DARKNESS

The giant scorpions shrieked as they attacked.

"Protect me, you idiot!" cried Ria.

Lifting his shield, Tom sprang towards the nearest of the hideous creatures. He spun his sword, slicing off snapping pincers. The scorpion screamed and the sting came darting down. Tom fended it off with his shield and stepped in close, stabbing into the middle of the scorpion's armoured back.

The blade pierced the hard segments and sank in deep. The scorpion's body convulsed and then exploded into a gush of black smoke.

They die easily – this is good!

Tom whirled around. Ria cowered against the wall of the tunnel, two more scorpions advancing on her.

"I'll save you!" he shouted, bounding along the tunnel. He hacked the two stingers off with one powerful sweep of his sword. Screeching, the scorpions turned on him, claws clacking, and their eyes alight with fury.

He jumped high as the pincers snapped, landing with one foot on the back of each of the creatures. Two swift stabs to the skulls and it was over. Black smoke puffed and swirled. The scorpions were gone.

"There are more!" yelled Ria, pointing.

Two scorpions were scuttling towards them. Tom sprang forward, swinging his sword. A pincer caught his blade and the creature tried to wrest the hilt out of his grip. The other scorpion scrambled up the wall and across the roof of the tunnel.

Tom struggled to free his sword, but the second creature was above

him now, its stinger dripping venom.
Tom lunged with his shield as the
long, curved tail darted at him. He
jerked his head back as the deadly

stinger struck the wood.

He yanked at his shield, dragging the scorpion down from the roof so that it crashed on to its back on the floor, its legs flailing, its tail still snagged on his shield.

Leaping high, he came down with both boots on the fallen scorpion's head. There was a horrible noise as the skull cracked and the creature exploded into a ball of black smoke.

One more to go!

Tom turned on the final scorpion. His arm ached with trying to free his sword. The pincers were like a vice and the scorpion was pulling at him with all its might, trying to get him within range of its lunging stinger.

Fine! We'll play your game...

Tom released his sword. Taken by surprise, the scorpion tumbled back across the tunnel. Tom ran after it, his shield in both hands as he smashed aside the tail and brought the rim down on the scorpion's thick neck.

The blunt head rolled, then a gust of smoke swirled around Tom's feet.

He picked up his sword and turned to Ria, breathing heavily.

"Nothing to it," he said.

Tom stared at Ria. Her eyes were wide, her mouth opening and closing silently. She was pointing at something above his head

Before he could turn, a weight landed on his back, and pain stabbed into his neck. Reeling, Tom flung himself backwards into the tunnel wall. There was a blast of smoke as the final creature was crushed between his armour and the rock.

Tom dropped to his knees in agony. Ria grabbed his hair and twisted his head to look at the wound.

"It's nothing," she said. "A scratch!"

"It must be poisoned," gasped Tom.

Ria snorted. "Some great hero you are," she said. "You've probably got hours to live yet." She let him go, and he fell back. "Come on, get up. You can still be helpful before you curl up and die."

Tom watched Ria march off down the tunnel, her cloak swirling.

There seemed to be two of her for a moment. He climbed to his feet, and followed quickly, blinking to clear his vision. The tunnel began to branch off in different directions. At each fork, Ria paused for a moment before picking a way forward.

"Wait for me," Tom told Ria, rubbing his eyes. Nothing helped. Everything was blurred. "There's something wrong with my eyes," he said. "I think it's the scorpion venom."

"Well, try not to go blind too quickly," Ria said. "I have work for you to do."

At another fork, Ria set off down one tunnel, but Tom called her back.

He could hear distant water.

He pointed. "We should go this way," he said.

"Why?"

"It feels right," Tom said.

Ria shrugged. "Very well – you're the Quester, after all. Just keep an eye out for danger. Ha! Get it? Because you can't see."

Tom was beginning to feel irritated by Ria. *If I can't see, I can't fight. She doesn't care at all!*

Tom led her along the tunnel, following the noise of the water.

"It seems you were right!" said Ria.

Even with blurry eyesight, Tom could see that they had entered a great cavern. Long stalactites jutted

over a vast lake of black water.
At the far side of the cave a dark
waterfall poured noisily down.

Tom saw an island of bare rock
jutting out of the middle of the lake.

"Is Fluger here?" he asked Ria.

"I think so," she said, giving him a shove. "Go and splash about in the water – that should wake him up."

"Let me heal my vision first," he said, taking the talon of Epos from his shield.

"If you must," said Ria impatiently.

Tom touched the talon to his forehead, hoping its healing powers would help him to see better. But as he did, he saw the water stir below.

"Something's there!" he cried. A dark, sinuous shape was approaching under the surface.

"I can't see anything," muttered Ria, peering past him. "Are you sure?"

Before Tom could move, a great thick tentacle whipped out of the lake, spraying him with icy water as it curled around his knees.

"Looks like Fluger has found you!" said Ria.

Tom cried out as he was torn off his feet and the talon flew from his grip. He reached for Ria, calling for help, but she refused to aid him. There was nothing he could do as he was dragged into the freezing water.

TERROR IN THE BLACK RIVER

"I can't see a thing," murmured Elenna.

It was pitch black at the bottom of the well. Far above them, the dim circle of sky was no larger than a coin.

Daltec said a few words in a strange language, and a slender blue flame appeared in the air between them. By its warm light, Elenna saw the mouth of a tunnel.

"Let me go first," she said, fitting an arrow to her bow.

A faint sound came from the tunnel mouth.

"I think that's moving water," she said. "An underground river, maybe?"

She moved cautiously into the tunnel. "Keep as quiet as you can."

She and Tom had entered many dark places in past Quests – and danger had always lurked in the deep shadows.

But this time Tom is one of the dangers!

Elenna paused at every curve and

bend, listening carefully, staring beyond the blue flame, poised for an attack.

The sound of rushing water grew louder all the time and turning a corner, Elenna was brought to a sudden halt. A river of black water rushed past her feet. A little way off she could hear a thunderous, pounding noise, echoing among the rocks.

It must be a waterfall!

Daltec's blue flame shone on the racing river, illuminating the far bank. *Too far to jump, and too fast to swim across.*

"There's no way to the other side," Elenna said, her spirits sinking.

"There may be," said Daltec. "Aduro taught me a very interesting spell during my apprenticeship. I've been waiting for the chance to use it."

He knelt at the edge of the river and dipped his fingers into the torrent of water.

"Be careful!" Elenna warned.

Daltec spoke a few curious words, and then stood up again. A loud crackling noise filled the tunnel and Elenna saw a patch of still, silvery water spreading out from the bank. It reminded her of something.

Ice on a windowpane!

"You've frozen it!" gasped Elenna as the sheet of ice sent long fingers

out across the width of the river.

"We must be quick," Daltec said. "The water is fierce and the spell is fragile."

Elenna stepped out on to the

glistening ice. It was firm under her feet, but slippery, and it was hard to move at speed. The blue flame showed movement at the river's edge. Cold dread flowed through Elenna's veins. Creatures scuttled about, long and low and yellowish-green. Curved tails rose above armoured backs. "Giant scorpions!" she cried.

The first of the creatures stepped cautiously on to the ice ahead.

"We have to go back," Elenna gasped.

"I think not," groaned Daltec. Elenna spun around, her heart pounding. More of the huge scorpions were approaching them across the ice from behind.

Elenna strung an arrow, but as she shifted her footing, she felt the ice crack under her. "Daltec, can you strengthen the spell?"

"Not for a while," he told her. "It takes too much energy – aargh!" The ice beneath his feet gave way and he plunged with a terrified yell into the seething river.

Elenna looped her bow over her shoulder and flung herself on to the splitting ice, reaching for the wizard's robes. She managed to snatch hold of his sleeve a moment before the ice cracked apart beneath her too.

The cold of the water was like

stabbing knives, and she let go
of Daltec. She struggled to keep
her head above the surface as the
current rolled her over. Taking a
desperate breath, she swam towards
the wizard. Daltec was flailing, and
sinking.

*His robes are too heavy. He'll
drown!*

Gasping for air, she managed to
grab his hood and haul his head
above the surface. He coughed and
spat out water, his frightened face
blue with cold already. His eyes
bulged.

Barely able to keep herself afloat,
Elenna manoeuvred behind him and
caught his chin in the crook of her

arm. She turned on her side, kicking
with her legs and swimming with
her free arm towards the bank. It
was no use. The power of the river
dragged her on and swept them
both helplessly over the lip of the

plunging waterfall.

Elenna somersaulted through the air for a few seconds then smacked into the surface of the river below. She was sucked beneath the churning torrent, but she still clung on to Daltec's hood. The water thundered down from above.

If I lose hold of him, he'll be pushed deeper!

Using every ounce of strength she possessed, she fought her way from under the waterfall to where the water was less turbulent. She saw a rocky bank not far off, and dragged Daltec along behind her. By the time Elenna hauled them both on to dry land, she was exhausted.

"I'm sorry I was so helpless," gasped Daltec. "I'm not used to such perils!"

"We survived," panted Elenna, giving him a faint smile. "That's all that matters." She felt in her pocket. The little vial with Aduro's antidote was still there. *Thank goodness!*

Now that Elenna's ears were clear of water, she could hear a strange thrashing sound. On her knees, she looked around.

They were in an immense cavern, on an island in the centre of a massive lake. Stalactites hung from the lofty roof of jagged shadows.

The thrashing came from the creature in the water. A huge,

sinuous Beast coiled and writhed. Its flesh was pale and flecked with uneven black stripes, and its long body was banded by razor-sharp fins. Its eyes were dark slits and its face was a mass of slithering, seething tentacles with hooked and barbed tips. At first Elenna couldn't tell why it tossed and flailed, but then she saw a body caught around the waist by several of the tentacles. *Tom!* He fought valiantly, stabbing at the Beast with his sword and parrying the slashing barbs with his shield, before the creature plunged him into the lake. The Beast's coils rolled in the frothing water and its tail flicked as it vanished.

An icy fist closed around Elenna's heart.

How can I defeat such a huge Beast? And how can I save Tom, if we can't fight side by side?

She drew an arrow. *I have to try!*

ENEMIES ON EVERY SIDE

The Beast's tentacles tightened their grip on Tom's body. He slashed at one with his sword. It reeled back, spraying blood, but instantly, another wrapped itself around his chest.

Fluger stank like rotting fish and foul water, and Tom's stomach heaved. His eyesight was so bad now that he could only see the blurred shape of Fluger's massive coils, flailing at the water.

Gritting his teeth, he hacked at the remaining tentacles, lifting his sword high and bringing it down with all his might. The pressure on his chest loosened a fraction.

It's working. The tentacles are weakening!

Another few blows of his sword and he would be free. But before Tom even had time to fill his lungs with air, Fluger whipped around and dived headfirst into the water, dragging Tom down.

The water roared in Tom's head.

He stabbed with his sword and
smashed the rim of his shield
down on the tentacles, kicking and

struggling with all his fading might.
But the Beast kept its grip on him.

I will not die like this!

Sheathing his blade, Tom grabbed
at the tentacles with his bare hands,
hoping that the magical power of
the black armour would give him
the strength to tear himself free. The
tentacles slithered in his hands, and
for every one that he managed to prise
free, another came snaking through
the water to grip him.

A shrill voice sounded in his
head. *Puny boy! You cannot win. I
am Fluger the Sightless Slitherer. I
devour all who come to my lair!* It was
the ruby of Torgor in his belt that let
Tom hear the Beast's jeering thoughts.

The pain in his chest was like burning coals, and his skull throbbed as though it would burst.

He grasped his shield in both hands and hammered its rim down between his breastplate and the tentacles. Then he levered the shield, using all the magic power of his armour, to push the tentacle loose.

Fluger's hissing voice filled with frustrated rage. *This cannot be!*

With a final burst of strength, Tom gained enough space to kick free. He swam for the surface, the last of his breath bursting from his chest. As his head broke into the fresh air, he sucked in great, gulping breaths.

But even as he filled his lungs, he

felt tentacles whip around his arms and legs. Fluger surfaced, sending up fountains of icy water as he lifted Tom high. Another tentacle tore his shield from his arm and flung it across the lake on to the shore.

Tom stared down in horror. A great gaping mouth appeared, ringed with rows of inward-facing teeth. The tentacles dragged him towards it. He managed to plant his feet either side of the monster's jaws, but the pressure tugging him was bone-breaking. However hard he tried, he couldn't break Fluger's deadly hold.

"Tom! I'm coming!"

He knew that voice – it was the
vile girl, Elenna.

He twisted his head and made out
a shape diving into the lake.

*So! She's in league with Fluger!
And now he's caught me, she's
coming for the kill!*

He tried one last time to drag
his limbs free, but Fluger was
too powerful. The rows of teeth
gnashed, eager to slice into his
flesh and drag him down into its
stomach.

I'm sorry, Ria. I've failed you.

Tom saw a grim look on Elenna's
face as she swam closer, an arrow
clutched in one hand.

*Yes! An arrow to the heart will
be quicker than a slow death in the
Beast's belly!*

He gasped in surprise as Elenna
suddenly darted to one side. Lifting

her arm, she plunged the arrowhead into Fluger's eye. The Beast's agonised scream lanced through Tom's mind.

Fluger thrashed wildly, his writhing tentacles releasing Tom. He spun dizzyingly through the air. He crashed into the lake, the impact stunning him. With no strength left, he sank into the water.

Then he felt something catch hold of him and haul him to the surface once more. He was a dead weight, his limbs refusing to obey any command, as Elenna pulled him in her wake towards the island in the centre of the lake.

She dragged him on to the rocky

shore. Still gasping for breath, Tom reached for the hilt of his sword. *If she thinks she can kill me while I'm weakened and half-blind, I'll make her pay.* He wrenched himself free of Elenna's grip and rounded on her, brandishing his blade.

"This is as good a place as any to kill you!" Tom shouted as he advanced on Elenna, rubbing at his eyes. She backed away as he swung his sword wildly. He must have missed, because the weight of the swing almost toppled him.

"Tom? Are you all right?" she said.

Tom pointed his sword at where he thought her chest was, but she was swimming in and out of focus. "I see

your plans well enough!" he said.
"You want to kill me yourself! That's
why you attacked the Beast!"

"No! I was saving you!"

He lunged at her, tripped, and fell to one knee.

"Listen, Tom," said another voice. *The wizard! Daltec!* "You're under an enchantment. Just a few drops from this vial will bring you back to your senses!"

Tom sensed the treacherous wizard approaching from the left. He lashed out an arm, and felt it connect with flesh. *Ha! Got you!*

He heard Daltec cry out "No! The antidote!" Then came the tinkling sound of broken glass.

"Tom!" Elenna cried in despair. "What have you done?"

"He's been a good and loyal

servant!" called a shrill voice from across the lake.

My lady!

Tom turned at the sound of Ria's voice. "I'm sorry," he called. "I failed you! The Beast was too strong! I can hardly see!"

"I noticed that," Ria shouted. "You were pathetic! Let's see what I can do!"

Dimly, Tom saw two purple beams shoot up from the far bank. Ria was using her sorcery to help him.

The beams of magic struck the stalactites above and Tom heard cracking noises. Peering at the scene, he could just make out rocks plunging down all around them.

"She's shattered the ceiling!" cried Elenna. "We'll be crushed!'

She pushed Tom aside as a shard of rock struck the ground where he had been standing. Tom lifted his sword to strike her, but bright light from above blinded him.

For a moment he thought he had been hit by a magical blast from Daltec, but then he realised that Ria's spell had broken through the roof. Rays of sunlight shot down, shimmering like silver on the water and lighting up the whole of the cavern.

Tom could just make out the Beast flailing around in the lake. The smell of scorching flesh filled his nostrils.

What's happening? If only I could see properly!

"Look!" shouted Elenna. "The sunlight is burning the Beast!"

Yes! Tom could smell the sizzling flesh as the Beast lurched and plunged in agony.

"I've weakened him for you," cried Ria. "Now finish Fluger off before I send down more rocks to crush you all like grapes!"

"Yes, my lady!" cried Tom, striding towards the water. Now he would be able to prove to his mistress that he was a worthy champion. But as he came to the lake's edge, Elenna sprang in front of him, her bow bent and an arrow aimed at his throat.

"Stop," she said grimly. "I won't let you past."

"You could never fire at me," Tom mocked. "You're too much of a weakling!"

KILL THE BEAST!

Elenna stepped back, her arrow still aimed just above Tom's breastplate. Her friend was blinking madly. The tight-fitting armour covered him from shoulder to toe, a dull black where it had once been bright gold. Looking into his face, it was still hard for her to believe how the blood of Krokol had turned his brave soul to evil.

She knew Tom was right – she couldn't fire an arrow at him – but perhaps there was still time to remind him of his true self.

"Listen to me, Tom!" she demanded. "Ria is not your friend."

He paused, staring at her, his sword drooping in his hand.

"Ria is evil!" Elenna cried. "You must know that in your heart."

Tom's jaw set firm, the moment of doubt and hesitation gone. "Out of my way, you liar!" he shouted, leaping forward and snatching the bow out of her hands. He flung it aside and shoved her roughly to the ground. "Once the Beast is dead, I'm coming back for you!"

"Daltec and I – we're your true friends," cried Elenna, ignoring the pain of her fall as she scrambled to her feet. "Please, Tom... You must remember the truth – fight the spell!"

Tom was at the water's edge now. But he paused, staring back at her, a look of confusion on his face again. He rubbed his eyes.

Elenna's heart was filled with pity. "You're remembering – I know you are!" she called to him.

"Elenna?" His voice was faint, puzzled.

"Yes!"

He's battling the enchantment!

Come on, Tom – you can do it!

A shudder went through Tom's body and his face hardened. "The Tom you knew was a weak-minded fool," he snarled. "I am glad to be rid of him!"

"No! That's Ria speaking – not you!" shouted Daltec.

Tom glared at him. "You pathetic excuse for a wizard!" he spat. "Ria has powers you cannot imagine!" He turned his back on them.

The spell is too strong. It's up to me to help him now. Tom was almost at the water's edge, preparing to dive into the lake. Elenna picked up her bow. "I'm so sorry!" she muttered. Her heart aching, she leaped forward and struck him on the back of the head with the weapon. He groaned, his knees buckling, and as he slumped down, she pulled him backwards so he wouldn't fall into the water.

Chunks and splinters of stone
were still falling, and the air was
filled with the stench of the Beast's
burning flesh as it sank beneath the
water and away from the light.

A plan was forming in Elenna's
mind as Ria's deadly bolts seared
above her. *She doesn't care if she
kills Tom at all. He's useless to her
now he cannot see.*

She took a rapid breath and
dived into the lake. Kicking fiercely
with her legs, she knifed through
the water, searching for the Beast
in the gloom below. She pulled an
arrow from her quiver, wondering
if she'd made the right decision.
This was the Beast's element, and

even if Fluger was hurt, he was still dangerous. Maybe even more so.

But her intention wasn't to fight one on one. She gripped the arrow in her fist.

It won't hurt him too badly – but it should anger him enough to make him follow me back to the island. She felt a moment of terrible uncertainty. *I hope I can swim fast enough not to be caught.* She pushed her fears away – there was no other choice!

She saw the shifting coils of Beast flesh not far beneath the dappled surface. *He's scared of the light. This is my chance!* Diving under the fins, she stabbed into Fluger's scaly flesh with her arrow.

The Beast shuddered and convulsed. Twisting in the water, Elenna tried to swim away, but she saw Fluger's long tail whipping towards her.

In desperation, she turned and clutched at the shaft of the arrow. She pulled herself out of reach as the tail smashed down. Fluger thrashed back and forth, and Elenna hung on grimly. Crashing waves slapped her face, the cold water blinding her as she fought to keep her grip. Fluger rose, lifting her helplessly into the air. More rays of daylight scorched the Beast's scales, filling the air with a foul stench. Elenna clung on to the arrow with all her strength. Then Fluger's long body curved downwards.

Elenna filled her lungs before the water hit her, clutching the arrow with both hands as she was almost ripped from Fluger's side. The water was dark and icy and the pressure was like a tightening band around her chest. She could just make out the rocky lake-bed beneath them. *Fluger is dragging me to the bottom!*

Suddenly the Beast turned on to its back. Elenna bit her lips to stifle a cry as Fluger smashed her into the floor of the lake. Pain exploded

through her body and for a horrible
moment she thought she would be
crushed between the Beast and the
rocks.

Fluger jerked suddenly upwards.

Elenna tried to cling on to the arrow, but the speed tore her hands away. She tumbled in freezing eddies, seeing the Beast spiral away from her through the murky water.

Her lungs screamed for air, her head almost bursting from the pressure. But she fought with all her remaining strength, struggling into less turbulent water and striking for the surface.

A shape clove the water above her. *Tom! He's come to help me!*

But Tom ignored her as he propelled himself ferociously through the water. Despair filled her heart as she realised his true purpose.

He's heading for the Beast...

DEATH IN DEEP WATER

Tom sped towards the Beast, the power of his magic leg armour propelling him down past Elenna into deeper water. Her tunic was torn from her encounter with the Beast, and she looked like she was struggling to get to the surface.

She'll probably drown. Good! That

will save me the effort of killing her later!

He held his sword out, the hilt gripped in both hands, the point of the blade aimed at Fluger's head. *I'll sink my sword in his skull to the very hilt! Then Ria will know I'm a worthy champion!*

Tom blinked in a futile attempt to clear his eyes. The Beast was a blur of writhing coils, moving fast through the water, racing away from him. He kicked out more violently, using every last bit of power in his legs to close in, then slashed at Fluger's tail. Black blood burst from a deep cut, billowing out through the water. The Beast's howl of pain

scorched his mind. Fluger jerked
his injured tail away, twisting in the
water in a tangle of scaly flesh.

Tom saw the Beast's tentacles
surging towards him, their barbed
ends eager to cut and slash.

Tom braced himself, and allowed the tentacles to twine around his body, biting into his skin. He gripped his sword tightly as he was pulled towards that great circular mouth.

The needle-sharp teeth parted, ready to crunch down on him.

At the last moment, Tom stabbed at the mouth. His sword slipped between the teeth and gouged tender flesh. Clouds of black blood spread into the water as the tentacles flung him away.

He had hoped to strike through the mouth and up into the brain. But all he had done was to anger the wounded Beast further. And his lungs were beginning to ache from lack of air. *Time to take a breath before heading back into the fray.*

Tom tried to swim to the surface, but a wall of flesh struck him. A thick coil looped around Tom's chest, clenching like a giant fist. He struggled, but it tightened further, squeezing his sword arm against his body.

I must get free or I'll drown!

Tom called on the power of his breastplate.

You will not kill me, Fluger! A Master of the Beasts never gives in!

Tom roared the last of his breath away in a stream of bubbles as he strained every muscle. The coil loosened at last, allowing him to

wriggle free. He jetted towards the
surface of the lake, and burst into the
air.

"Tom! You may not trust me, but
I can help you!"

He turned in the water, to see

Elenna – or the shape of her, at least – back on the island.

So she survived, curse her!

"Never!" Tom shouted.

"You're almost blind," Elenna returned. "The Beast will kill you! Swim back here before it's too late!"

Beneath him Tom could hear the water currents churning as Fluger surged upwards.

With a growl of frustration, he realised King Hugo's lackey girl was right. Without his shield and hardly able to see, how could he hope to fight such a powerful Beast? He sheathed his sword and swam for the island, a new idea rising from his Evil heart.

Maybe she does have her uses. She can help me defeat the Beast, and then, when the fight has weakened her, I can finish her off!

He saw a tall figure standing on a high point of the island. *It must be that treacherous wizard, Daltec.*

But what was he doing?

The wizard raised his arms and Tom heard chanting. Bursts of blue fire erupted from Daltec's fingertips, blazing up towards the remains of the roof.

Tom heard a rushing noise from behind. Fluger had surfaced! The enraged Beast was racing through the water, mouth agape.

Tom fought to pull himself

towards the island, swimming until his shoulders burned. But Fluger was closing in.

I'm not going to make it...

Above the pounding of his heart and the thrashing water, Tom heard a cracking sound, reverberating through the cavern.

Elenna's voice rang out across the water. "Tom! Watch out!"

Splintered stones splashed into the water all around him. More of the roof was coming down!

With a desperate look back, he saw Fluger lunging, the tentacles reaching out. Tom gasped in pain as they wrapped around his waist and pulled him back with a bone-wrenching jerk.

That stupid girl distracted me! That was her plan all along!

A much louder and deeper crack sounded from the roof. Tom stared up and saw a huge stalactite plunge

downwards like a falling dagger point. It struck Fluger's body just behind his head, ripping through flesh and muscle and bone. Blood fountained up as the tentacles slipped away from Tom, and the

Beast sank beneath the lake, leaving the surface churning with eddies.

Through the raging water, Tom could see Fluger shrivelling and dissolving away to nothing. He grinned with joy and slapped the water with his hands. Fluger was dead!

As the surface stilled again, something floated up, bobbing nearby. It was a single glittering scale, all that remained of the Sightless Slitherer.

Ria's voice rang out. "Grab it, you fool!" Tom swam over, snatched the scale, then struck out for the island.

As he reached its shore, Elenna there, reaching out to help him.

Tom took her hand, and let her pull him from the water. As soon as he had two feet on dry land, he snaked an arm around her middle from behind, and placed his blade against her neck.

"Tom!" she gasped. "Daltec and I saved you!"

"More fool you!" Tom snarled. He stared up at Daltec. "Try any of your magic on me, and I'll cut her throat!" he called.

"Tom, fight the spell," Daltec urged. "Remember who you are."

Tom sneered at him. "What spell, you snivelling sorcerer?"

The sound of clapping came across the lake. "Oh, very well

done," called Ria, her voice dripping sarcasm. "What a team you make!"

"We *are* a team," Elenna whispered to Tom. "We always have been."

"Lies!" spat Tom. "Just more pathetic lies!"

Ria called again, her voice hardening. "Tom – don't waste your time on her. Come to me. Now!"

Tom took his sword from Elenna's throat and shoved her to her knees. He had to obey Ria – he *wanted* to obey.

"I'm coming, my lady!" he cried.

He paced across the island then turned and ran. Calling on the mighty power of his magical leg our, he reached the water's edge and leaped. Soaring over the lake he landed lightly at Ria's side.

"Hand it over," she said.

Tom dropped to one knee in front of her and placed Fluger's scale in her hand. Despite his blurred vision,

he could see a smile of victory widen on her face.

"Have I done well, my lady?" he asked.

She shrugged. "You were adequate," she replied. "Now – hold still while I deal with your eyesight." She grabbed his hair and tilted his head to one side. He saw that she was holding the talon of Epos that had been torn from his hand when Fluger had first attacked. "This should do the trick!" She placed the magical talon to his temple.

Tom felt a searing pain like lightning running through his skull. He let out a cry, screwing his eyes up in agony.

"Don't be such a weakling!" Ria said. "Open your eyes!"

Tom blinked. He could see the lake and the cavern perfectly. Sunlight poured through the broken roof from a clear blue sky. It was wonderful!

"Thank you, my lady," he gasped, getting to his feet.

"If it had been hard, I wouldn't have bothered," Ria replied.

Tom stared across the lake to the island where Elenna and Daltec stood. Their faces were miserable – they looked utterly defeated. The girl even had tears in her eyes.

She always was weak! Now perhaps she'll understand that my allegiance lies with Ria!

"Let's bring this to an end!" Ria said casually. She lifted her arm and a bolt of purple magic sprang from her fingers. It struck the remains of the broken roof above the island. Rocks and rubble rained down.

Tom saw a look of shock on the faces of his two enemies as they were engulfed in the debris, clinging to one another like cowering wretches. He heard cries of terror, suddenly cut short. The rumble of falling rock died away. Dust rose over the island and drifted across the lake.

"There," said Ria, dusting her hands together. "That's that! And here comes our ride."

As though she had silently

summoned him, Ria's flying horse came swooping down out of the sky. Its hooves struck the rock with a clatter as it drew up beside them, folding its wings along its sides.

"Good boy," Ria said, stroking the horse's neck. "Ever faithful, just like my pet Beast killer." She patted Tom on the head. "Help me up, will you?"

Tom crouched and offered his hands. Ria placed a booted foot on them, and hoisted herself up on to the horse's back. Tom climbed on behind.

As they rose, Tom glanced down to the smoke-shrouded island. The crushed bodies of his enemies lay under the rubble, finally defeated.

Remembering for a moment the sadness in Elenna's face, he felt the briefest prick of regret that Ria had needed to kill her and the wizard. But an inner glow drowned out his sympathy.

Our enemies are gone – and we're well on the way to achieving our goal.

The stallion burst out into bright daylight, his wings pounding the warm desert air. The ruined village lay behind them and ahead the rolling desert dunes stretched away to the distant horizon.

Tom smiled.

Life as Ria's loyal champion is rather fun!

CONGRATULATIONS, YOU HAVE COMPLETED THIS QUEST!

At the end of each chapter you were awarded a special gold coin. The QUEST in this book was worth an amazing 8 coins.

Look at the Beast Quest totem picture opposite to see how far you've come in your journey to become

MASTER OF THE BEASTS.

The more books you read, the more coins you will collect!

Do you want your own Beast Quest Totem?

1. Cut out and collect the coin below
2. Go to the Beast Quest website
3. Download and print out your totem
4. Add your coin to the totem

www.beastquest.co.uk

READ THE BOOKS, COLLECT THE COINS!
EARN COINS FOR EVERY CHAPTER YOU READ!

550+ COINS
MASTER OF THE BEASTS

410 COINS
HERO

350 COINS
WARRIOR

230 COINS
KNIGHT

180 COINS
SQUIRE

44 COINS
PAGE

8 COINS
APPRENTICE

550+
515
480
445
410
395
380
365
350
320
290
260
230
217
206
191
180
146
112
78
44
30
19
8

READ ALL THE BOOKS IN SERIES 24:
BLOOD OF THE BEAST!

Meet three new heroes with the power to tame the Beasts!

Amy, Charlie and Sam – three children from our world – are about to discover the powerful legacy that binds them together.

They are descendants of the *Guardians of Avantia*, an elite group of heroes trained by Tom himself.

Now the time has come for a new generation to unlock the power of the Beasts and fulfil their destiny.

Read on for a sneak peek at how the Guardians first left Avantia by magic…

Karita of Banquise gazed in awe at Tom, Avantia's mighty, bearded Master of the Beasts.

Under his leadership, she and her companions would today face their greatest challenge.

Tom pointed towards the brooding Gorgonian castle. "We must recover the chest of Beast Eggs Malvel stole," he reminded them. His fierce blue eyes moved from Karita to the others. Dell of Stonewin, whose bloodline connected him to Beasts of Fire; Fern of Errinel, linked to Storm Beasts; Gustus of Colton, bonded with Water Beasts.

"Malvel will be expecting an attack," Tom said. "His power is lessened, but he is still formidable." His eyes locked on Karita. "Stealth will be our greatest ally."

Karita felt as though her whole life had been a preparation for this moment. Countless hours spent studying the ancient tomes, day after day of gruelling combat training, months learning how to influence the will of Stealth Beasts and control the powers that filled the Arcane Band at her wrist.

But was she ready?

She gazed into Tom's face, and her doubts faded.

Yes!

A low rumble came from the

castle. Flashes of green lightning shot from the clouds as a swarm of screeching creatures erupted from the battlements.

Karita shuddered as Malvel's hideous minions streaked through the sky. They were man-sized, with white hides, limbs tipped with hooked claws and gaping jaws lined with sharp teeth. Their leathery wings cracked like whips.

"Karrakhs!" muttered Tom. "Karita – go!"

She nodded and slipped away behind jagged rocks. She turned to see the swarm of foul creatures engulf her companions. Tom's sword flashed. Howls rang out from the Karrakhs. The Guardians were using their Arcane Bands to form weapons that spun and slashed!

Karita raced for the castle, keeping low behind the ridge of rocks. Reaching the walls, she climbed up a gnarled vine and found a narrow window to crawl through. She looked back again. Tom and the Guardians had battled their way through the castle gates.

Well fought!

She dropped into a room and crept to the door. Torches burned in the corridor, casting shadows. The castle was silent, but Karita felt a growing dread as she slipped along the walls.

She knew where the chest of Beast eggs was hidden. But would Malvel allow her to get to them?

She came to a circular room, and saw the chest standing by the wall. Her heart hammering, Karita opened the lid and gazed down at the eggs. They were different sizes, shapes and colours. One slipped from the pile and she caught it in her gloved hand. It was pale blue, about the size of a goose egg. Acting on instinct, she slipped it inside her breastplate.

Crash!

She spun around. Malvel stood against the room's closed door.

"Did you really think you could enter my domain unseen?" he snarled, a green glow igniting in his palm. His voice was weaker than she'd imagined. "I *wanted* you to come here. After all, only a Guardian can hatch a Beast Egg."

Karita swallowed hard, seeking a way to escape.

"You and your friends will hatch these Beasts and I will drink in their power," growled the wizard. "I will become mighty again and Avantia will bow before me!"

"I'm not afraid of you!" Karita shouted.

A ball of green fire exploded from Malvel's hand. Karita dived aside, seared by the heat.

She leaped up, thrusting her right arm towards the wizard. The Arcane Band began to form a weapon, but another blast of fire sent her sliding across the floor.

Malvel loomed over her, both hands

burning green. Before he could strike, the door burst open and Tom and the Guardians rushed into the room.

"No!" roared Malvel. "Where are my Karrakhs?"

"Defeated!" shouted Tom, whirling his sword to deflect Malvel's green flames. "Guardians! Take the eggs!"

Fern dived for the chest, but a blast from the wizard knocked her over.

"The eggs are mine!" howled Malvel. He traced a large circle of fire in the air. There was a blast of hot wind as the flaming hoop crackled and spat.

Malvel snatched up the chest and turned to the heart of the fiery circle.

"He's opened a portal!" shouted

Tom. "Stop him!"

Gustus ran at the wizard and wrested the chest from his grip. Roaring in anger, Malvel launched a fireball, but Fern managed to shove Gustus out of its path. But the force of her push knocked Gustus into the portal. With a stifled cry, he and the chest of eggs were gone.

"No!" Fern shouted, diving in after him. With a yell, Dell ran after her.

"Wait!" shouted Tom.

"It's our duty to protect the eggs!" Dell called back as he disappeared into the swirling portal.

Malvel sprang forward, but Tom bounded in front of him, holding him back with his spinning blade as the wizard hurled magical fireballs.

Karita saw the walls of the portal writhing and distorting. Malvel's fireballs were making it unstable. At any moment it might vanish!

Tom was knocked back by a torrent of green fire as the wizard turned and leaped into the portal. Karita flung herself after him.

"No! Karita!" The last thing she heard was Tom's voice. "The portal is in flux! You could be sent anywhere!"

And then there was nothing but a rushing wind and howling darkness, as she plunged into the unknown.

Look out for
Beast Quest: New Blood
to find out what happens next!